Moral Stories

LESSONS FOR LIFE

An imprint of Om Books International

Reprinted in 2018

Om
KIDZ

An imprint of Om Books International

Corporate & Editorial Office
A 12, Sector 64, Noida 201 301
Uttar Pradesh, India
Phone: +91 120 477 4100
Email: editorial@ombooks.com
Website: www.ombooksinternational.com

Sales Office
107, Darya Ganj, New Delhi 110 002, India
Phone: +91 11 4000 9000
Fax: +91 11 2327 8091
Email: sales@ombooks.com
Website: www.ombooks.com

ISBN : 978-93-81607-19-0

Printed in India

10 9 8 7 6 5

Contents

The Clever Fox and the Goat

One summer afternoon, a fox was walking in the forest. The sun was shining hot and bright in the sky and the fox began to feel thirsty. He went round and round the trees, looked in the bushes and sniffed all around. And ah-ha! There it was — a big, deep well of water! The fox was so happy that he jumped right into the well and gulped down so much water that his tummy was ready to burst.

Now that he had finished drinking water, the fox decided to get out of the well and go on his way. So he looked around for a way to climb out and saw that there was none! Every time he tried to go up, he would slip down. He tried and he tried, but with no luck.

"Oh! Someone please help me! Get me out of here!" The fox cried from the well, hoping that someone would hear him and come to save him. Many hours went by but nobody crossed the well. "It seems I'll be stuck here forever," thought the fox, sadly.

The day turned into evening and soon the sky was dark. The poor fox spent the night in the cold and damp well. He was very scared because he did not know how long it would be before someone would come and help him get out of the well. Time passed by very slowly.

At long last, it was morning. "Somebody, help me!" the fox began to shout once again. And this time, his prayers were answered. Luckily, a goat happened to be crossing the well just as the fox shouted for help.

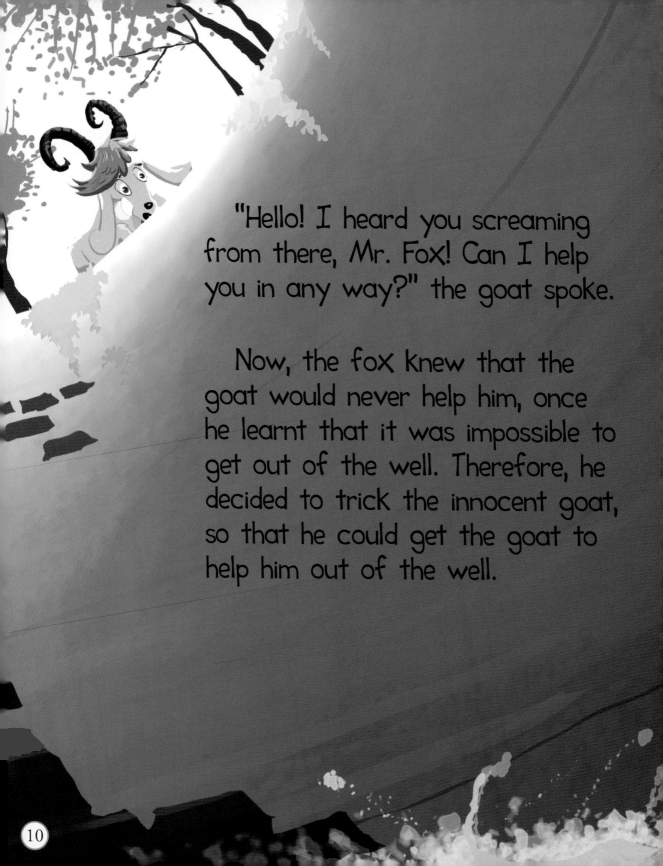

"Hello! I heard you screaming from there, Mr. Fox! Can I help you in any way?" the goat spoke.

Now, the fox knew that the goat would never help him, once he learnt that it was impossible to get out of the well. Therefore, he decided to trick the innocent goat, so that he could get the goat to help him out of the well.

"I came down into this well to drink this cool, refreshing water. Believe me, my dear goat, I have never ever tasted water quite like this. Why don't you come down and drink some too?" said the sly fox.

The goat, on hearing the fox, was overjoyed and at once she jumped into the well and was beside the fox. But as soon as the goat finished drinking the water, she too realized that getting out of the well was impossible.

The fox was very clever. He thought of a plan to escape. "Why don't you stand on your hind legs, and I'll climb over you to get out of the well. Once I am out, I shall pull you out too!"

The goat was pleased, since the fox's solution appeared to be the best way out. Without wasting another moment, the goat stood up with her hands against the wall of the well. The fox immediately jumped over the goat's back and climbed out, free at last!

But as soon as the fox was out of the well, he started walking away without looking back even once. The goat started crying to the fox for help.

"Mr. Fox, you had promised to help me get out of the well too!" she screamed.

But the fox merely replied, "Listen, my friend! If you had been smart, you would not have leaped into the well before seeing if there was a way out!" And so saying, the fox started walking away to his own house and the poor goat was left in the well.

Moral: Look before you leap.

The Tortoise and the Hare

One day in the forest, the hare was having a good time, making fun of the tortoise. "Ha ha ha! Look how funny your hands and feet are, my good friend Tortoise! No wonder you walk so slow."

The tortoise was very angry at the hare for making fun of him. "Stop making fun of me, Hare! I may be slow, but I always finish what I have started!"

But that just made the hare laugh even more. "I am sure you finish whatever you start my friend, but you just take sooooooo long! It's really funny to see you doing the same thing for many, many days."

"Why don't we have a race, Hare? That will be the best way to know who is the faster between the two of us!" said the angry tortoise.

"Ha Ha!" laughed the hare, "you must be joking, friend Tortoise! How could you even think of defeating me in a race? You should know that it is just not possible for you to run faster than me!"

But the tortoise had been insulted
enough. He had to prove, once and
for all, that he was not slow.

The two arguing friends went to the
fox, the smartest creature in the forest,
so that he could fix the path
of the race. The fox was
most helpful, and soon
it was time for the
tortoise and the hare
to start their race.

As soon as the fox
yelled "Go", the hare
ran so fast that all one
could see was a large
puff of dust behind him.
He had to show the
tortoise that he was
the faster of the two
of them.

The poor tortoise, on the other hand, could not even get a good start. By the time he could go a little ahead of the starting line, the hare was nowhere to be seen.

The hare kept running and running, and soon he had almost covered half of the track. As he kept running, he turned around to see where the tortoise was, and realizing that the tortoise was nowhere to be seen, he decided to slow down for a while.

"Ha! That foolish tortoise actually thought that he could run faster than me. Here I am, halfway through the race, and he must still be at the starting line!" thought the hare to himself.

He decided to take some rest, since he was certain that the tortoise would take a long time to catch up to him. He spotted some green grass nearby and walked over there to eat some of it.

After a short while, having eaten a lot of the delicious green grass, the hare began to feel sleepy. He thought he was definitely going to win this race and so there would be no harm in sleeping for a little bit. The hare dozed off under a huge, shady tree, very happy with himself.

Meanwhile, the tortoise had kept walking. He was getting very tired, but he kept telling himself that he could not stop and rest. After all, the hare was already so far ahead of him. He kept walking and walking, and soon reached the spot where the hare was taking a nap.

He could see his friend, the hare, fast asleep, but that did not stop the tortoise. He just kept walking and walking and did not bother to stop and rest even for a little while.

The hare woke up after a long time. He still had to finish the race! He looked around to see where the tortoise was but couldn't spot him anywhere. "Oh, he must be far behind me," he thought and skipped along on his way to the end of the race.

As soon as he could see the finish line, he saw that he had been wrong! The tortoise was already present there and had won the race!

The hare never made fun of the tortoise's slow speed again.

Moral: Slow and steady wins the race.

The Goose that Laid Golden Eggs

Once upon a time in a place far, far away, there lived a poor farmer with his wife. They had nothing but a little farm where they grew vegetables that they could eat.

One day, the farmer's wife said to him, "Wouldn't it be nice if we could have some eggs once in a while? I wish we had a goose to lay us eggs everyday!" The farmer didn't have much money to buy a goose. So, he gathered some vegetables and set off to the market to sell them and maybe get a goose in return.

He came back to the farm in the evening, carrying a goose. His wife was very happy and couldn't sleep all night, waiting for the goose to lay its first egg.

Morning came and
the farmer went to the
barn to get the egg.
And what did he find?
A golden egg! He found
an egg of gold!

The farmer began to dance and sing a merry tune, so happy was he. The goose, too, began to cackle loudly. Hearing all the noise, the farmer's wife came rushing to the barn.

"Look, my dear!" said the farmer, "See what the goose laid for us."

"A golden egg!" exclaimed the wife, clapping her hands, "This is a magical goose. We could soon be very rich!"

The next day was the
same again, and the next
and the one after that. The
goose laid a golden egg
every day.

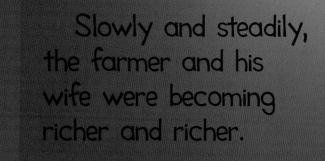

Slowly and steadily,
the farmer and his
wife were becoming
richer and richer.

Soon, a time came when the farmer and his wife just couldn't wait for one single egg every day. They wanted all the eggs right away.

"This goose must have a lot of golden eggs inside itself," said the wife to the farmer, "Why don't we just take them out all at once?"

"You are right, my dear," he said, and so saying, he cut open the goose's tummy to get all the eggs at once!

But there were no eggs inside! The goose could only lay one egg a day!

Alas! Now the farmer and his wife had lost the goose and they would never get any golden eggs again.

Moral: Too much greed always leads to great loss.

The Hungry Fox and the Shepherds

In a land far away, there was a very pretty pasture at the end of the forest. Shepherds from all over would bring their flock to that pasture. While the sheep would graze, the shepherds would all sit down and spend time with each other, telling stories or just playing games.

Now, the shepherds would remain at the pasture with their flock for nearly the whole day and therefore, it was necessary for them to bring their afternoon lunches with them.

But the shepherds were concerned about where they would keep their lunch, before eating at noon. They knew that if they left their food anywhere, wild animals would smell their lunches and steal their meals.

They knew that they had to look for some safe place to store their lunch, till they would all sit together and eat. They kept searching the entire pasture and finally came to the end of the grassland.

There the shepherds spotted a tree, which had a huge hollow in the trunk. However, there was a very narrow opening in the trunk of the tree, from where one could reach into the hollow inside the tree.

The shepherds decided that the hollow in the tree trunk would be the best place for them to hide their lunches, as no wild animal in the forest would be able to reach down through the narrow opening and grab their food.

Since then, the shepherds would always gather at the pasture every morning and after letting their sheep loose to graze around the pasture, they would all store their lunches in the hollow of the tree, before settling down to play games with each other.

One day, a hungry fox was passing through the edge of the forest. The poor fox had not eaten for many days, and was looking everywhere for some food. He had grown very thin and all his bones were showing.

As he was walking past the edge of the pasture, he could smell the delicious lunches that the shepherds had stored in the hollow of the tree trunk. Without wasting another moment, the fox ran straight towards the tree, so as to eat the shepherds' lunch.

As soon as he got to the tree, he could see how the shepherds had very cleverly used the small opening to reach the hollow of the trunk. Since the fox had not eaten in a long time, he was thin enough to walk straight through the narrow opening and enter the hollow tree trunk.

None of the shepherds realized
that the fox was inside the tree and
was happily eating all the food that
he could find there. And the fox just
went on eating and eating and eating.

After some time, all the food was
gone and the fox was finally full! He
was very satisfied and decide to leave
before the shepherds came to get their
lunches out.

But alas! After eating all that food, the fox was no longer thin. And however much he tried, he just could not fit through the narrow opening of the tree trunk. He had managed to get in because he was very thin then, but after eating so much food, it was not possible for him to get out!

The poor fox was stuck. He just kept sitting in the trunk and prayed very hard, hoping that the angry shepherds would not beat him up for stealing their food.

Moral: Excess is bad.

The Ungrateful Traveller

One day, two travellers were walking along a dusty road. It was a very hot day and there was not a spot of shade anywhere. The travellers could find no place to sit down and rest.

They just kept walking and walking, with nothing but the dusty road in front of them. Finally, after walking for a long, long distance, they were finally able to spot one tree in the far distance.

It was a huge tree, with such thick and leafy branches that they spread themselves around the trunk like an umbrella. There was a huge shade under the tree, more than enough space for the two travellers to rest peacefully and stretch their legs for a while.

The tired travellers
finally reached the tree
and sat down under its
cool shade.

They stayed in the shade of the tree for quite some time and were well-rested. Once they had cooled off, one of the travellers looked up at the tree. After studying the tree's features for quite some time, the traveller remarked to his companion, "Ah, look at this tree — it's so huge and yet it bears no fruit!"

His friend too looked at the tree and observed how the tree did not have any fruit on its branches. But he replied, "It does not matter, my friend! I am thankful that the tree has provided us this much-needed shade rather than fruit."

However, the first traveller was not convinced. He said, "Still, I do not see why this tree should be there at all if it cannot bear any fruit! After all, what good is a tree if it is not good enough to bear fruit?"

As soon as the traveller spoke these words, there was a very loud rustling of leaves and branches. The sound was so loud that the two men were scared out of their wits. They looked up, trying to see what was making that sound.

But before the two travellers could make any sense out of what was happening, they heard someone speak.

"So you would prefer it if I gave you fruit and not shade?"

The travellers were now very scared. The first traveller whispered, "Who is that? Who is speaking?"

"It is I, the tree, under whose shade you have come to rest. But you are not satisfied with that, are you? You want more, you ungrateful person!"

The first traveller
was very scared now,
and yet, at the same
time he was also very
ashamed. He realized
what the tree was
trying to tell him.

He stood up very slowly and said, "I am sorry, O great tree! I have been very ungrateful far the comfort that you have given me. From now on, I shall always remember to repay someone with gratitude!"

The tree was happy that the traveller had learnt his lesson and the two travellers rested under the tree for a long time before they were on their way again.

Moral: Always be grateful to others for their help.